# Storyland
## CLASSICS

Retold by Howard Hall

*Illustrated by Rene Cloke*

AWARD PUBLICATIONS LIMITED

# The Three Little Pigs

There were three little pigs called Grunter, Porker and Squeaky who lived on a farm. All the animals on the farm lived happily together until one day the farmer sold the farm.

"What shall we do?" cried Porker.

"We'll just have to leave and build homes for ourselves!" replied Squeaky.

So the three little pigs went off to pack their bags. As they said goodbye to their friends the sheepdog warned, "Watch out for wicked Grey Wolf!"

Carrying their bags, the three little pigs
walked down the farm track into the
countryside.

Now Porker had always liked the smell of fresh straw. He liked the smell so much he decided that he would build his house out of straw. So he left his friends and went to see a corn farmer who sold him some bundles of straw, enough to build a house.

Porker soon set to work. The straw was light and easy to carry. By noon the house was finished, but he'd been so busy, he didn't see Grey Wolf come creeping along.

With one big puff
the wolf blew Porker's
house down.

Meanwhile, Grunter and Squeaky were walking by the wood. They hadn't walked very far when they met a boy selling sticks.

"That's given me an idea," said Grunter. "I think I'll build my house out of sticks."

"Good luck! I'll come and visit you soon," cried Squeaky.

With the help of two fieldmice, Grunter built his house out of sticks. He worked so hard that his house was almost finished by dinner-time. He had just painted the front door when Grey Wolf crept out of the woods.

"Three puffs and I'll eat you for dinner!" growled Grey Wolf.

Grunter locked the door in fright. But Grey Wolf blew. And the third time he blew, poor Grunter's house fell down.

Grunter ran away as fast as his legs could carry him.

Only Squeaky remembered the sheepdog's warning about Grey Wolf. So he built his house with bricks and mortar. He carefully cemented the bricks together so that the walls of his house were thick and strong.

Two little songbirds sang beautiful melodies as he built his house of brick.

It was growing dark by the time Squeaky had finished. He was really glad to lock the front door and go upstairs to bed. He had just put out the light when there was a knock on the door. He opened the window and looked out . . .

Squeaky shivered with fright when he saw Grey Wolf standing on the garden path.

"What do you want?" he asked.

"May I come in?" asked the wolf, licking his lips.

"No, you can't," answered Squeaky.

"But I'm very hungry," said the wolf.

"I have no food for wolves," replied Squeaky. "Only turnips."

"Turnips?" cried the crafty wolf . . .

"If it's turnips you like," said the wolf, "I know a turnip field by the rabbit warren. The turnips there are delicious. Why not meet me there at seven o'clock tomorrow morning?"

"All right, Mr Wolf," yawned Squeaky. "I'll meet you there at seven."

Licking his lips, the wolf crept away. "At seven I'll have a nice tasty pig for breakfast," he chuckled.

Of course, Squeaky didn't want to see the nasty wolf again. So he stayed in bed until ten o'clock.

When Squeaky arrived at the turnip field
the wolf had gone, and Squeaky was able to
eat two nice turnips in peace.

Later he made friends with some rabbits
who told him where he could find some
delicious apples. "You'll find them in the old
orchard where the red squirrels live," they
said.

"In the afternoon I'll go to the orchard,"
decided Squeaky. "I only hope I don't meet
the wolf there."

Squeaky was sitting
in the orchard eating
an apple when the
wolf came. But
before the wolf
could even lick his
lips, Squeaky threw
him an apple.

"Try an apple, Mr
Wolf," he squeaked.
"They're really
delicious."

As the wolf turned to chase the apple, Squeaky slid down the tree and ran all the way home.

Squeaky was very pleased with his new home. He soon made friends with all the squirrels and rabbits and the songbirds in the neighbourhood. But he really missed his old pals Grunter and Porker.

"I hope Grunter and Porker will visit me soon," he said. "We'll have so much to talk about."

One day when the fair came to a nearby hill, Squeaky decided to go.

"I might meet Porker and Grunter there," he said, "unless that nasty Grey Wolf has gobbled them up."

Squeaky had a lovely time at the fair. As he rode on the roundabout he forgot all about the nasty wolf. He even won a balloon and a wooden barrel to keep his turnips in.

"It's just what I needed," he squeaked. "What a wonderful day it has been."

Squeaky was singing a song and carrying his
barrel home, when he had a horrible fright.
Just ahead of him he saw Grey Wolf.

The wolf was climbing up the hill towards
the fair. In a second or two he would see
Squeaky. Squeaky was so scared he let go of
his balloon!

For a moment poor Squeaky just stood there. What could he do? It was almost too late to hide.

Then Squeaky had a clever idea. He climbed into the barrel and put on the lid. Slowly the turnip barrel began to roll towards the wolf . . .

Once the turnip barrel reached the hill it rolled faster and faster. And what is more, it rolled straight towards Grey Wolf.

"It's chasing me!" growled the wolf. "I'd better run." So the wolf ran off down the hill.

The barrel travelled so fast at one point that it flew through the air, frightening the wolf even more.

At the bottom of the hill, the wooden barrel stopped. Squeaky lifted off the lid and crawled out. Grey Wolf was nowhere to be seen.

"I've just frightened the wolf!" laughed Squeaky.

"You frightened me too, Squeaky," cried a rabbit. "And once Grey Wolf hears it was you inside the barrel, he'll be very angry." But for once Squeaky didn't care.

When Squeaky arrived home he could have danced with joy. Porker and Grunter had arrived! They were standing in the garden waiting for him.

"Grey Wolf blew our houses down," they explained. "He would have eaten us too if he'd caught us. And we're so glad you're safe and well."

"You must both stay here," said Squeaky. "The wolf can't blow this house down because it's made of bricks and mortar."

"But he's sure to come back when he knows there are *three* pigs here," said Porker.

"Then we must lock the door and keep the windows tightly shut," said Squeaky. "And cheer up. I've gathered some turnips. If you light the fire, Porker, we can have a nice turnip soup. Then we can talk about our adventures since we left the farm."

The big soup pot was bubbling on the fire and the three little pigs were looking forward to their meal. They had forgotten all about the wolf when there was a loud knock on the door.

"It's the wolf!" yelped Porker.

"He's come to eat us," grunted Grunter.

"What do you want, Mr Wolf?" asked Squeaky.

"I want to come in," growled the wolf. "You must let me in. I'm very hungry."

"You can't come in," said Squeaky.

"If you don't open the door," warned the wolf, "I'll climb onto the roof and come down the chimney pot!"

The next moment the three little pigs heard the wolf climbing onto the roof. Then they heard him growl down the chimney pot.

"The chimney pot!" squealed Porker. "He's coming down the chimney pot. And we'll be eaten alive!"

The pigs listened as the wolf began to climb down the chimney. Porker and Grunter were frozen with terror. In a second or two the wolf would be in the room and they'd all be eaten alive.

But at the very last moment, Squeaky walked to the fireplace. As the wolf appeared, Squeaky lifted the lid off the soup pot.

The nasty Grey Wolf dropped straight into the boiling soup. "That's the end of the wolf!" squeaked Squeaky.

It was the end of the wolf – but not the
end of the three little pigs.

Grunter and Porker built their houses next
to Squeaky's, and every Friday night they
cook themselves a big pot of turnip soup.

# The Three Bears

As Goldilocks walked through the woods one morning she smelled a delicious smell. Someone was cooking porridge, and Goldilocks loved porridge.

Goldilocks didn't know that three bears lived in the wood and it was their porridge she could smell.

The three bears lived in a great big hollow tree. It was so big inside the tree that the three bears had made their home there.

Mother Bear had just served up the porridge when Father Bear said, "Let's go for a short walk. When we get back the porridge will be ready to eat."

"That's a very good idea," agreed Mother Bear. "And I can collect some berries on the way."

So off they plodded. Big Daddy Bear in front, followed by medium sized Mummy Bear, followed by tiny little Baby Bear.

A few moments later, Goldilocks came to the great big tree where the three bears lived.

Goldilocks had never seen a front door in a tree before. She was so curious that she opened the tree door and stepped inside the house of the three bears . . .

On the kitchen
table were the three
bowls of porridge.
There was a big
bowl. A medium
sized bowl. And a
tiny wee bowl.

Seeing the bowls of steaming porridge made Goldilocks feel very hungry. She was so hungry that she tried a spoonful of the porridge in the big bowl. But it was much too salty.

Next, Goldilocks tried the medium sized bowl. This porridge was too sweet.

Last of all, Goldilocks tried the porridge in the tiny bowl.

Goldilocks liked the taste of the porridge in the tiny bowl. In fact it was so delicious that Goldilocks ate it all!

Then she thought, "I wonder whose house this is? I wonder whose porridge I have been eating?"

Goldilocks walked into another room in the three bears' house and saw a great big chair.

"I'm so tired," sighed Goldilocks. "I think I'll sit down in this chair." But the big chair was Father Bear's chair and it was much too big for Goldilocks. "I wonder if I can find a smaller chair," sighed Goldilocks.

In another room inside the hollow tree, Goldilocks found a medium sized chair. This chair belonged to Mother Bear. In the room was a window with a lovely view of the woods.

"It will be nice to sit here," said Goldilocks. "I can look out of the window." But when she sat on the medium sized chair she found that it was very hard.

"Perhaps there is a softer chair somewhere," she sighed.

In little Baby Bear's room, Goldilocks found a tiny chair. It was soft too. What's more, Goldilocks found it very pleasant to sit on.

But Goldilocks was too heavy for the tiny chair . . .

The chair broke and Goldilocks fell on the floor! She was lucky not to hurt herself.

Goldilocks picked herself
up and started up the stairs.
She was so sorry to have
broken the little chair. But
she was still very tired.

"I wonder what is up these stairs?" she thought to herself. "Perhaps I might find a bed there to lie on."

It really was the strangest house Goldilocks had ever been in. Who would believe her if she said she had been in a lovely house inside a great big tree? Some of the branches of the tree actually grew inside the house.

On the wall by the stairs were ornaments, some of brass and some of china. The stairs were nice and clean and everything smelled as fresh as a forest on a spring day.

As Goldilocks climbed the stairs she was beginning to wish she lived in such a pleasant house.

She was yawning as she came to a green door right at the top. Having walked so far and eaten such nice porridge, she was feeling very sleepy indeed. All she wanted to do now was to lie down and rest . . .

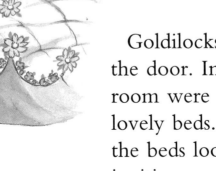

Goldilocks opened
the door. Inside the
room were three
lovely beds. Each of
the beds looked so
inviting.

There was a big bed. A medium sized bed.
And a tiny little bed.

Each of the beds was covered in a beautiful
eiderdown that had been made by Mother
Bear.

The big bed belonged to Father Bear. The
medium sized bed belonged to Mother Bear.
And the tiny little bed belonged to Baby
Bear.

Goldilocks tried the big bed first, but it was too hard.

So Goldilocks tried the medium sized bed. But it was too soft.

Finally, Goldilocks lay down on the little bed. It was just right! It was just like her bed at home.

There was a cuddly teddy bear sitting at the top of the little bed. As Goldilocks closed her eyes she wondered whose teddy bear it was. And whose bed she was lying in . . .

Only a few moments passed before Goldilocks fell into a deep sleep in Baby Bear's bed.

Meanwhile, the three bears were on their way home. They had had a very pleasant walk in the woods and now they were all looking forward to their breakfast.

"Our porridge should be ready to eat by now," said Father Bear in his big deep voice.

Father Bear had found a stout walking stick in the wood and he was very pleased with it. "This is just what I've been looking for," he boomed.

"Yes," said Mother Bear in a softer voice. "And I've found these lovely coloured berries to hang over the fireplace. Won't they look nice?"

"Yes, they will," squeaked Baby Bear in his tiny voice. "And I've found a wooden hoop which I will put in my playroom."

Suddenly Father Bear stopped. The door of their tree house was standing open . . .

"I'm sure I closed the door when we left. I do believe that someone has been inside our house!" growled Father Bear.

"I wonder who it can be?" Mother Bear said anxiously.

"I do hope they haven't eaten my porridge, because I'm very hungry," said Baby Bear.

But someone *had* eaten Baby Bear's porridge. And that wasn't all!

"Someone has been sitting in my chair," boomed Father Bear.

"And in my chair too," said Mother Bear.

"Oh!" cried Baby Bear. "Someone has been sitting in my chair. And, look, they've broken it!"

"Who can it be?" gasped Mother Bear. "Who has eaten Baby Bear's porridge and broken Baby Bear's chair?"

The three bears were gathered round Baby Bear's chair when, suddenly, Father Bear heard a noise upstairs . . .

"Someone is in the house," boomed Father Bear. "Someone is in our bedroom!"

"I do hope they're not sleeping in my bed," cried Mother Bear.

"And I hope they haven't hurt my teddy bear," squeaked Baby Bear.

Father Bear opened the bedroom door and
the three bears saw Goldilocks sitting sleepily
on Baby Bear's bed. She had been woken up
by Father Bear's deep voice.

"Who are you?" asked Mother Bear. "And
why are you sleeping in Baby Bear's bed?"

Goldilocks was so frightened. She had
never seen a *real* bear before! So she ran
quickly past the three bears, hurried down
the stairs and out of the door.

The three bears just
stood and stared.
They couldn't
believe their eyes!

No one, apart
from Uncle Bear,
had ever been in their
house before.
"She must have eaten
my porridge," said
Baby Bear.
"And broken your chair," boomed Father
Bear.

Goldilocks ran,
and ran, and ran.
She ran as fast as
her legs could
carry her.

Goldilocks didn't stop running until she was nearly home. It would be the last time she would walk into someone else's house without being asked. And of course, Goldilocks told no one where she had been, for no one would believe a tale about three bears who lived in a tree!

As for the three bears . . .

They made some more porridge. And mended Baby Bear's chair. And lived happily ever after in their secret home in the great big tree.

# The Adventures of
# Tom Thumb

"Last night I dreamed we had a child,"
sighed the farmer's wife. "But he was no
bigger than a pencil!"

"I'd not mind if he were no bigger than
my thumb," cried the farmer. "If only we
had a child."

In the twinkling of an eye, a tiny boy
appeared in the farmer's hand. The boy was
no bigger than the farmer's thumb, and he'd
been sent to them from heaven!

The happy farmer's wife
made the boy a bed out
of a pea pod and clothes
out of coloured ribbons.

The farmer made the child coloured balls
out of dried peas and a boat out of a walnut
shell.

The farmer and his wife were so happy
with their gift from heaven. And they called
their tiny child Tom Thumb.

One bright day the farmer had to take his horse and cart to market to fetch some hay, but he wasn't feeling too well. His wife told him to rest but the farmer said, "I *must* take the horse and cart to market today. It is very important."

Suddenly Tom Thumb piped up. "Sit me in the horse's ear," he said, "and I will drive the horse to market. When I want the horse to stop I'll shout 'Whoa!' And when I want the horse to trot, I'll shout 'Giddy-up!'"

So the farmer sat Tom in the horse's ear. The people who saw the cart passing by couldn't believe their eyes. They thought the horse and cart were being driven by magic!

Tom Thumb drove the cart all the way to market and back home again.

The farmer's wife was so pleased with her tiny child that she baked him a tiny cake.

One day two men
saw Tom Thumb
sitting on a toadstool
near the farmer who
was chopping wood.

"I'll give you a
gold coin for the
tiny imp," offered
one man.

The farmer was about to refuse but Tom said, "Please let me go. It will be an adventure for me. Later I'll escape and come back home to you."

So the man gave the farmer a gold coin, picked up Tom and set him on his hat-brim. Tom had a fine view from the hat-brim as the men walked along. But when he heard that the men were going to sell him at the fair, Tom grew frightened. So when the tall man took off his hat, Tom jumped off the hat-brim and ran away.

Tom ran as fast as he could through the tall grass. How he wished he could stride along like a tall man!

As the sun grew hot he found his way into a mousehole, which seemed as big as a cave to Tom. Here he made friends with a mouse who gave him some wild corn to eat. Later Tom rested before continuing his journey home.

Tom's bedroom during
the night was an empty
snail's shell which sheltered
him from the wind. He
used an old leaf as a
mattress, and found it very
comfortable.

The next day, after
a long walk, Tom
Thumb arrived home.
The farmer and his wife were so pleased to
see Tom. But later in the day Tom had an
accident. He was climbing upon the table
when he slid down a spoon into the pudding
basin. The farmer's wife didn't see Tom and
put the pudding in
the bag!

Next the farmer's wife put the pudding bag into the cooking pot which was simmering on the fire. Tom began to jump up and down inside the pudding bag. It was so hot. The farmer's wife, not knowing that Tom was inside, thought that there was something wrong with the pudding so she gave it to a passing tramp.

Luckily, Tom was able to escape when the tramp opened the bag. And by evening he was back again with the farmer and his wife.

One fine day, the farmer's wife took Tom
with her when she went to milk the cows.

The sky was blue and the wind was scented with summer flowers. It was a beautiful day.

The farmer's wife was worried that a cow might accidentally tread on Tom so she tied him to a thistle with a piece of ribbon. Tom enjoyed sitting there in the soft breeze. The thistle gently rocked in the wind like a swing and Tom grew sleepy. The farmer's wife seemed to be taking such a long time.

Eventually Tom fell asleep and he dreamed he was going to have a great adventure . . . Later he woke and began to sing a song. His voice sounded like a silver flute and one of the cows pricked up its ears at such a lovely sound.

As the thistle swayed to and fro and Tom sang, a beautiful blue butterfly came along. It, too, had heard Tom singing and liked the sound. So the blue butterfly hovered near Tom as he sang, and listened to the song.

Tom smiled
at the butterfly,
and the butterfly
smiled back
at Tom.

Then a friendly cow came along to where Tom was sitting on the thistle.

"Please can you teach me to sing?" said the cow.

"I'll try," said Tom. "But first you'll need to think of a tune you'd like to sing."

"Very well," said the cow. "I think I'd like to sing 'Hey Diddle Diddle'." But when the cow opened its mouth to sing it blew Tom straight off the thistle and into the grass!

As Tom Thumb scampered through the
grass looking for the farmer's wife, an eagle
saw him. Now, Tom looked as small as a
mouse to the eagle, so the eagle swooped
down and plucked Tom out of the grass.
Suddenly Tom felt himself flying through the
air at great speed.

The eagle flew on and on, until Tom could see the sea below. "Help! Please put me down," cried Tom. The eagle was so amazed to hear him speak that he dropped Tom in surprise. Poor Tom fell with a splash straight into the sea. The water was very deep and very cold.

"Help!" cried Tom. "I can't swim."

Tom swallowed lots of salty water and he felt himself sinking. "I'm drowning," he thought. "I'll never see the farmer or his wife again. I do wish I hadn't tried to teach that cow to sing. And I wish I could be saved just this once." As Tom was thinking that, he was swallowed by a great big fish! Inside it was dark and cold. But at least it was dry.

Tom didn't feel very well at all. He had swallowed so much water, and now it was cold and dark. Tom was just about to take his boots off when the fish he was in was caught by a fisherman on the shore.

Suddenly the fish was flying through the air towards the shore.

Inside the fish, Tom closed his eyes. Everything was so quiet and still and it was very dark. Tom tried shouting for help but no one came to rescue him.

Then Tom began to feel frightened. He imagined he was in a dungeon at the bottom of the sea. He began to shiver. It was certainly cold enough to be a dungeon.

After a time, poor Tom began to feel very weary. So he lay down inside the fish and after a long time he fell asleep.

Meanwhile, the big fish had been taken to a fishmonger's. But when the fishmonger saw the big fish he said, "This is a fish fit for a king to eat." And he had the big fish sent at once to the palace.

That evening the King's cook began to prepare the royal meal. The King's cook had just cut open the fish when Tom Thumb woke up. When Tom climbed out of the fish the cook couldn't believe his eyes!

"My goodness! Who are you?" cried the cook. "I've never seen anyone so small in all my life!"

"My name is Tom Thumb," said Tom. "And who, may I ask, are you?"

"I'm the King's cook," said the man. "And you've just climbed out of the King's fish. I must show you to the King and Queen."

The cook put Tom on a plate and took him before the King and Queen. "Excuse me, Your Majesties," said the cook. "But look what I've found inside the royal fish."

The Queen clapped her hands with delight as Tom bowed to the royal family. And the King said, "Well, bless my soul!" over and over again.

Tom bowed again. "Good King and
Queen," he said, "my name is Tom Thumb.
I'm the son of a poor farmer and his wife
who live many miles from here."

Tom went on. "I've had lots of adventures.
I've dined with a mouse and I've sat in the
ear of a horse. But now I'd just like to go
home, please."

"And so you shall," promised the King.

"Thank you very much, Your Majesty," said Tom.

The king invited the farmer and his wife to the palace to collect Tom, and gave him a doll's-house to live in as a special present.

Later, Tom Thumb entertained the royal children, and told them all about his adventures, and the following day he returned home with the happy farmer and his wife.

# Puss In Boots

There was once a miller who had three sons:
Peter, John and Robin.

When the miller died he left his money to
Peter. His mill he left to John. To his
youngest son, Robin, he left only a cat.

This cat's name was Puss. And Puss was a
very special cat.

"You're a nice old cat," said Robin to Puss. "But how am I going to feed us both? I have no money and no job."

"I may be able to help," purred Puss. "But I'll need a pair of boots and a hat. One last thing," added Puss. "Get me an old sack too. Then just leave everything to me."

Robin found a hat for Puss, and a sack.

And with his last few coins he bought Puss some yellow boots.

The very next day Puss went for a walk
with the sack over his shoulder. As he
walked he tried to think of a plan.

On his way he saw a piece of rope lying
near a rabbit warren.

"That's given me an idea,"
said Puss. "All I need now
is a stick and a sprig
of parsley."

Within an hour Puss had
found a stick and a sprig of
parsley.

Puss in Boots stopped by a tree. Inside the sack he put the sprig of parsley. Puss kept the bag open with the stick. And to the stick he tied the rope. Then he hid behind the tree.

A woodpecker perched in the tree couldn't understand what Puss was doing. So he waited to see what would happen next.

Soon three rabbits came bobbing along.
The first rabbit stopped near the sack.

"I can smell parsley,"
he said.

"No use just smelling
it," said the second
rabbit. "Let's eat it!"

The three rabbits
crept inside the bag
and nibbled the
parsley.

Puss waited until
they were all inside,
then he pulled the
rope and caught all
three rabbits in the
sack.

After combing the feather in his hat, Puss polished his yellow boots. Then he lifted the sack full of rabbits over his shoulder.

"Now, my next plan is to go to see the King," he purred to himself. "I've heard His Majesty is very fond of rabbits."

When Puss had walked to the palace, he knocked at the gate, and because the guards hadn't seen a cat in boots before, they let him in.

Next, Puss saw one of the King's ministers who didn't know what to make of a puss in boots.

Finally, Puss was taken in to see the King.

Puss took off his hat and bowed very low before speaking.

"Your Majesty," he purred. "I have been sent on a very special mission by my master, the Marquis of Carabas. He sends his respectful greetings, and asks me to bring you a small gift."

Puss opened the bag with the rabbits inside. The King smiled when he saw the rabbits.

"Well," said the King. "Thank your master for his gift. The rabbits will be most welcome and here is a gold coin for yourself."

That night Puss in Boots slept in a barn. He didn't bother going home to see Robin because he wanted to stay near the palace.

The next day Puss in Boots bought himself a coat, and then made another trap, using the same stick, rope and sack.

He set the trap in the woods, and inside the sack Puss sprinkled some grains of golden corn. He took one end of the rope and hid behind a tree. Two plump woodpigeons saw the corn, and when they entered the sack to feed, Puss tugged on the rope and caught the birds in the sack.

Next, Puss sent the woodpigeons to the King, with a note which read:

*To the King, from the Marquis of Carabas.*

Later Puss heard that the King was to make a journey in his royal carriage with the Princess, the beautiful Rose-Marie. Puss made his plans . . .

"The Marquis of Carabas must come with me at once," cried the King. "I will give him a fresh change of clothing."

"Your Majesty is so kind," purred Puss, bowing low.

When Robin was dressed in royal clothes, he looked just like a young prince. And when he bowed to Princess Rose-Marie she fell in love with him.

"I'm proud to know the Marquis of Carabas," she said with a smile.

Robin really didn't know what to say. He only hoped Puss knew what he was doing. But Puss was a clever cat. He was already planning his next move.

In fact, even as Robin was changing into dry clothes, Puss was running on ahead of the carriage. He ran until he came upon some workers in the fields.

"If anyone passes by in a carriage," cried Puss, "please tell them that these fields belong to the Marquis of Carabas. You'll be rewarded if you say that."

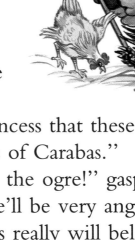

Puss ran on until he came upon a farmer.

"If the royal carriage passes by," said Puss, "tell the King and Princess that these fields belong to the Marquis of Carabas."

"But they belong to the ogre!" gasped the farmer. "If he hears he'll be very angry."

"Tonight these fields really will belong to the Marquis of Carabas," promised Puss. "So please do what I ask."

"Very well," agreed the farmer, "but I hope you know what you are doing."

Puss ran on through a wood until he reached the castle where the wicked ogre lived. Everyone lived in fear of the ogre. It was said that he had the power to change himself into any creature he chose.

Puss was running up the steps of the castle when the gigantic figure of the ogre loomed ahead. The ogre carried a great big club and glared at Puss as if he would eat him for supper.

"Hello, Mr Ogre," said Puss.

"Who are you?" growled the ogre. "And what is more to the point – what do you want?"

"Oh, I'm just an ordinary cat," said Puss. "But I heard that you were a very clever man."

"I *am* a very clever man," boomed the ogre. "I'm the cleverest man in the whole world! I'm also the nastiest, and the biggest, and last, but not least; I'm also a magician."

"A magician!" gasped Puss. "I've always wanted to meet a magician. Can you make things disappear, and can you pull rabbits out of a hat?"

"Any magician can do that," growled the ogre. "But *I* can change myself into a rabbit, or even a tiger! In fact, I can do anything I want to do!"

"I'll bet you can't change yourself into a mouse," sneered Puss.

"Of course I can change myself into a mouse. What colour mouse would you like?"

"Oh, any colour will do," said Puss.

"Right! Just you watch," the ogre said, laughing. "Just you watch."

There was a puff of smoke and the ogre vanished. Puss heard a tiny voice and looked down and saw that the ogre had changed himself into a brown mouse.

"You see," squeaked the mouse, "I can change myself into anything. That is why everyone is frightened of me."

Quick as a flash, before the ogre could change back again, Puss killed the mouse.

The ogre was dead!

"This castle now belongs to the Marquis of Carabas," cried Puss.

Puss hurried up the steps into the kitchen.
When the servants of the castle heard that the
ogre was dead they were much relieved.

"He was a cruel master," said the butler.

"Well, now you have a new master,"
purred Puss. "His name is the Marquis of
Carabas. You'll find that the Marquis of
Carabas will be a good and kind master, I
promise you."

"In the next few minutes," continued Puss, "the royal carriage will arrive at this castle. Will you please lay on a feast fit for the King and his lovely daughter Princess Rose-Marie, and the Marquis."

When the food was almost ready, Puss reminded the servants, "Remember, your new master will arrive soon. And his name is the Marquis of Carabas."

When the King arrived
with the Princess and
Robin, Puss in Boots was
there to greet them.
"Welcome to the castle of
the Marquis of Carabas,"
he purred.

Robin was amazed. Puss seemed to be
taking care of everything. And the King and
the Princess were happy to accept Robin as
the Marquis of Carabas.

Robin and the Princess were so deeply in love that they had eyes only for each other. They often went out walking together.

One day Robin asked Princess Rose-Marie to marry him and she accepted gladly.

Within a year they were married and the Marquis of Carabas became Prince Robin. And Puss, wearing his favourite boots, was the first bride's cat; taking the place of a bridesmaid!

Of course Robin and his Princess lived happily ever after.

And as for Puss in Boots? Well . . .

He was given some royal boots and a royal jacket. He ate royal fish, and drank royal cream. He slept in a royal cat basket, and chased royal mice.

Some time later, Puss married too. And the kingdom was blessed with royal kittens.

# Snow White and the Seven Dwarfs

In the heart of a forest stood an old castle.

In the castle lived a king and queen. They had a lovely baby daughter called Snow White, but the Queen was always worried about Snow White's health. One day, as the Queen was sewing a bonnet for Snow White, she pricked her finger with the needle. As the Queen looked at the drop of blood on her finger she made a wish.

"May our daughter Snow White grow into a beautiful child. May her hair be as dark as a raven, and her skin be as white as snow."

Snow White did grow into a lovely
But sadly, the Queen died when Snow
White was still a baby.

Later, the King
married again. This
Queen was beautiful,
but vain. She was
also wicked, and had
once been a witch.
She had a magic
mirror which she
often asked:

"Mirror, mirror,
on the wall, who is
fairest of us all?"

The mirror always
answered, "You are
fairest, my Queen."

One day the Queen asked her mirror, "Who is fairest of us all?"

The mirror answered, "Snow White is fairest of you all."

At first the Queen couldn't believe what she had heard.

But the mirror repeated, "Snow White is fairest of you all."

The wicked Queen was so angry.

In a rage, she ordered a woodcutter to take Snow White into the forest and kill her.

Fortunately the woodcutter was a kindly man. He had no wish to harm a hair on Snow White's lovely head. So he told Snow White to run away and hide from the wicked Queen, and never to go near the palace again.

After saying goodbye to the woodcutter, Snow White walked through the forest. She walked and walked until she was a long way from the castle.

On her journey she made friends with the animals. The birds brought her berries and nuts to eat. But as the day wore on, Snow White grew worried. She didn't know where she was going to shelter for the night.

As it grew dark, Snow White felt very tired. She was just about to lie down beneath a tree, when she came to a tiny cottage, almost hidden under a hawthorn tree.

Snow White walked wearily up the short path to the front door of the tiny cottage. She knocked quietly on the door. In her hand she carried a gift of flowers.

When no one answered, Snow White opened the door and stepped inside. She entered a small room.

Round the table were seven little chairs. Upon the table were seven little cups.

"Who can live here?" gasped Snow White.

Snow White wanted to sit down, but most of the chairs seemed too small. She didn't know what to do. So she went into another room and found a small bed.

"I do hope no one will mind if I lie down here," she said. She didn't know that the little cottage belonged to seven dwarfs.

As she lay on the bed, some of her animal friends came to keep her company. Within a minute, Snow White was fast asleep.

The dwarfs mined gold in the secret
mountains. They worked every day, except
Sunday. And, even as Snow White slept, they
were marching home for tea.

The dwarfs were friendly with the animals
too. But when a rabbit came to tell them that
they had a visitor called Princess Snow
White, the dwarfs didn't believe him.

The dwarfs arrived back at their cottage in the forest and got a surprise. The rabbit had told the truth. They did have a visitor, and her skin was as white as snow.

The dwarfs just stood and stared at the beautiful Princess. For a time no one spoke.

Snow White began to wake. "I must be dreaming!" she cried as she opened her eyes and saw the dwarfs standing there.

"Fear not," whispered the eldest dwarf. "We will not harm you. Tell us what has brought you to our home in the forest, and we will try to help you."

"I am a princess," explained Snow White. "But my stepmother wants to kill me! I walked through the forest all day looking for somewhere to rest and finally found your cottage. Please will you help me?"

"You must be Princess Snow White!" said one of the dwarfs. "A rabbit told us about you. Don't worry. We will shelter you from the wicked Queen, and take care of you."

Snow White cooked for the seven dwarfs and kept their cottage clean and tidy.

They built a chair and bed specially for her and brought her little gifts carved from wood and stone. In the evenings they all sat by the fireside and the dwarfs told tales of the secret mountain and of trees that could talk.

After a time, Snow White forgot her fear of the wicked Queen.

A month passed. Then one
day, when Snow White was
alone in the cottage, who
should come stealing through the woods but
the wicked Queen. Once again she had asked
the magic mirror who was the fairest. When
it had replied, "Snow White is fairest," the
jealous Queen knew that Snow White was
still alive.

As the Queen passed through the forest,
even the trees looked unhappy. Animals fled
in fear. Some of the animals were going to
try to warn Snow White, but the power of
the wicked Queen stopped them.

When the wicked Queen came to Snow
White's window, she was disguised as an old
woman. She carried a basket full of ribbons.

"Here's a pretty red ribbon for your dress,"
she cried to Snow White. "Come out and let
me tie it for you."

"You're very kind," smiled Snow White.
"But I'm afraid I can't afford to buy a
ribbon."

"You may have the ribbon," insisted the wicked Queen. "I have plenty."

"Thank you," smiled Snow White. "The red ribbon is so pretty."

"Here, let me tie the ribbon for you," repeated the disguised Queen.

So Snow White let the Queen tie the ribbon to her bodice. But the Queen tied the ribbon so horribly tight that Snow White could hardly breathe. She fell to the ground, dying. Luckily, the seven dwarfs came home early and saved her life by cutting the ribbon.

The wicked Queen came back the next day. This time she was disguised as a gypsy woman. She tapped on Snow White's window. "Look, my dear, I have a pretty comb for you," she crooned.

Snow White opened the window. "The dwarfs told me to stay indoors," she said.

"Don't worry," muttered the Queen. "I can place the comb in your hair from here." So saying, the Queen placed the comb in Snow White's hair, but the comb was poisoned. As soon as it touched Snow White's head, she fell to the ground.

When the dwarfs returned they found Snow White dying. But when the eldest dwarf saw the strange comb in her hair he grew suspicious. As soon as he removed the comb, Snow White quickly recovered.

"The comb was poisoned," he explained.

"You've saved my life again," said Snow White, smiling. "How can I ever thank you all?"

The next day, before the dwarfs set off for work, the eldest dwarf gave a warning to Snow White.

"The wicked Queen is sure to know that you are still alive. So you must be very careful. If any strangers come to the cottage you must not speak to them. Keep all the windows and doors locked. And let no one in."

Snow White promised to be careful.

The dwarfs set out for work in a happy mood, thinking that Snow White would be safe. But the wicked Queen came back, this time disguised as an apple seller.

One of the apples looked so red and juicy, but in fact one half of the apple was poisoned. The jealous Queen offered the apple to Snow White.

"Thank you," smiled Snow White, "but I'd rather not eat it."

"Why ever not, my dear?" cried the sly Queen. "There's nothing wrong with it. I'll take a bite myself to prove it to you."

The Queen took a bite from the good half of the apple. Then she handed the apple to Snow White. "Take a bite from the other side, my dear," said the wicked Queen. "You'll find it's the nicest apple you've ever tasted."

Snow White took the apple. "Thank you," she smiled. "I love apples, and I'm sure this apple will be delicious."

"Of course it will, my dear," muttered the evil Queen.

Snow White took one bite from the poisoned half of the apple and fell to the floor as if dead.

Her animal friends sent a fast-flying bird to fetch the dwarfs, who hurried home as fast as they could.

When the seven dwarfs arrived, they used all the herbs and medicines they knew to try and cure Snow White. But Snow White did not recover. She just lay silent on the ground.

"She's dead," said the eldest dwarf at last.

A great sadness hung over the little cottage.

The seven dwarfs made plans for Snow White's funeral. They were all very upset, but there was work to be done.

They decided that Snow White should be buried in a hilltop garden, which lay among the secret mountains.

The dwarfs made a glass coffin for Snow White and laid her inside. The animals decided to take scented flowers to brighten her grave.

On the day of the funeral, the dwarfs set out carrying the glass coffin. It was a long journey. Nevertheless, many of the animals went along to pay their last respects to their friend Snow White.

On the way to the secret mountains, a handsome prince rode past. When the Prince saw the beautiful Snow White lying in the glass coffin, he asked the dwarfs to stop. One of the dwarfs slipped, and the coffin banged hard on the ground.

This upset the dwarfs; but the sudden jolt made the piece of poisoned apple fall out of Snow White's throat!

Snow White awoke, as if
from a deep sleep. The handsome
Prince kissed Princess Snow
White's hand. The dwarfs and
the animals were so delighted!

What started as a funeral
procession was soon to
be a wedding between
the Prince and their
beloved Snow White.

For the wedding, the
seven dwarfs brought
gifts of gold and silver
from their mine in the
secret mountains.

The animals came to the
wedding bringing fruit and flowers.
And Snow White and the Prince had a truly
happy life together.

As for the wicked Queen . . .

Well, she grew tired of looking in the
magic mirror. All her wicked deeds had made
her very ugly indeed.

# Aladdin and his Wonderful Lamp

A long time ago in China there lived a little boy called Aladdin. His father had died when Aladdin was just a baby. So his mother had to bring him up alone.

Aladdin lived with his mother in a tiny hut on the outskirts of the city. In the distance they could see the many roofs of the Emperor's palace.

Aladdin's mother was one of the Emperor's washerwomen. Aladdin did his best to help his mother. He would collect bundles of dirty laundry from the palace for her to wash. When the laundry was clean and dry he'd take it back to the palace.

Sometimes he would get a glimpse of the Emperor's daughter, whom he liked very much. He sometimes saw the Emperor's daughter walking in the palace gardens. But it is unlikely that she ever saw Aladdin.

Although Aladdin and his mother worked hard, they were still very poor. The roof of their hut leaked when it rained. And at times they barely had enough rice to eat.

Aladdin often dreamed of having a nice house, and he promised his mother that one day they would have a fine home. But his mother just smiled. Aladdin also dreamed of marrying the Emperor's daughter!

One day, when Aladdin was out walking, he met a strange-looking man, who said to him, "You are called Aladdin."

"That's right!" said Aladdin. "But how did you know my name?"

"I am a magician!" said the man. "And with my magic I can give you and your mother all the riches you ever dreamed of."

This is what Aladdin had been longing to hear. "I would like my mother to live in a fine house," said Aladdin.

"Good," said the magician. "But to earn your riches you must come with me into a secret cave in the mountains. In the cave is a precious lamp. I want you to go into the secret cave and fetch me that precious lamp."

Only the pure in heart could enter the secret cave. That is why the magician had sent Aladdin!

In the cave Aladdin saw many treasures. Just for fun he tried on a golden ring, but when the magician saw this he hissed, "Quick! Give me that precious lamp, or I'll leave you in the cave to die."

"No, please help me out first," begged
Aladdin. "Then I'll give you the lamp."

But the magician was furious. He closed up
the cave, leaving Aladdin inside to die.

"I'm trapped," thought Aladdin. "There's
no way out. I'll never see my poor mother
again." Aladdin sat down on the stone floor
and began to cry. He twisted his hands
together and as he did so he rubbed the ring
on his finger. The ring was a magic ring.

There was a puff of smoke and a figure appeared before Aladdin.

"I am the Spirit of the Ring," said the figure. "What is your wish?"

"Please take me home," begged Aladdin. "And let me take the precious lamp with me." In an instant, he found himself back home.

Aladdin put the precious lamp in his
mother's room. Then he went out into the
garden to await her return. He still had the
magic ring on his finger, so he wished for a
glimpse of the Emperor's daughter. The
Spirit of the Ring granted his wish.

Just for a moment he saw the Emperor's daughter, walking in the palace gardens. And it seemed to Aladdin that she was more beautiful than ever.

Later, when Aladdin showed his mother the lamp, she said, "It doesn't look like a precious lamp to me. And what is more, it needs a jolly good clean." So she went to the drawer and took out a cloth.

As Aladdin's mother polished the lamp, there was a bright flash of light followed by a loud bang, like a clap of thunder! A huge golden figure appeared before them, saying, "I am the Genie of the Lamp. What is your command?" Aladdin's mother gasped.

"Now I know why the magician wanted the lamp. It's a magic lamp!" said Aladdin.

The Genie of the Lamp waited until Aladdin and his mother could think of something to wish for. Finally, Aladdin and his mother asked for great riches, and a grand house with servants and nice food to eat.

"And make sure the roof doesn't leak," added Aladdin.

"Your wish is granted," cried the Genie. In a moment, Aladdin found himself dressed in silk and his mother in the finest satin.

After a few days Aladdin invited the Emperor's daughter to tea.

They fell in love, and one day Aladdin
went to the palace and asked the Emperor if
he could marry the Princess. He took the
Emperor a tribute of gold and silver. The
Emperor, who also liked Aladdin, gave his
consent to the marriage.

Aladdin and his Princess settled down and
lived happily together in Aladdin's palace.

Then one day the magician returned. He was dressed as a pedlar, shouting, "New lamps for old!" It was a trick to get the precious lamp.

Aladdin was out, but a servant girl heard the call.

She brought down the magic lamp and exchanged it for a shiny tin lamp.

As soon as the magician saw the lamp, he knew it was the magic lamp from the treasure cave.

"At last I've found it," he hissed. "How Aladdin escaped from the cave, I'll never know. But now I'll turn him into a laundry boy again." After saying this the magician rubbed the lamp.

When the Genie of the Lamp appeared, the magician said, "Take the Princess, and Aladdin's palace, and me, to darkest Africa!"

"Your wish is my command," said the Genie. In a very few moments, Aladdin's palace, with the Princess and the magician inside, had landed in darkest Africa.

"This will teach Aladdin to meddle with magic," said the magician, with a laugh. "When he sees that his palace has vanished, he'll wonder if he's been dreaming."

When Aladdin came home he found that his palace had disappeared into thin air. His Princess was nowhere to be seen.

Aladdin sat down and began to cry. He could not understand what had happened. Perhaps it had all been a dream?

But after a time, Aladdin remembered the magic ring that was still on his finger. So he rubbed it, and the Spirit of the Ring appeared.

"What is your
wish?" asked the Spirit
of the Ring.

"Please take me to my
Princess," pleaded Aladdin.
And off they went.

The Princess was overjoyed to see Aladdin. "I never thought I'd see you again!" she cried.

Aladdin asked her what had happened.

She explained, "The magician has got the magic lamp. He made a wish, and we flew here from China. It was most amazing!"

Aladdin hid until the magician was asleep. Then he crept up and took back the lamp. When he rubbed it the Genie asked once again, "What is your command?"

"Take the Princess, the palace, and me back to China," said Aladdin.

"What about the magician?" asked the Genie.

"Please leave him here," said the Princess.

The Genie of the
Lamp granted their
wish.

Suddenly Aladdin and his Princess found
themselves back in their palace in China. The
first thing Aladdin did was to hide the
precious magic lamp.

When the magician
woke up, he was all
alone in Africa.

"Oh dear!" he sighed.
"That's the trouble with
magic, you never know
what will happen next."

ISBN 978-1-84135-520-7

This edition first published 2007

Published by Award Publications Limited,
The Old Riding School, The Welbeck Estate,
Worksop, Nottinghamshire, S80 3LR

3 5 7 9 10 8 6 4 2
10 12 14 16 18 20 19 17 15 13 11 09

Printed in Malaysia